In a Creepy, Creepy Place and Other Scary Stories

Also by Judith Gorog:

**IN A MESSY, MESSY ROOM
AND OTHER SCARY STORIES**

In a Creepy, Creepy Place and Other Scary Stories

By Judith Gorog
Illustrations by Kimberly Bulcken Root

Harper Trophy®
A Division of HarperCollins Publishers

Harper Trophy® is a registered trademark of
HarperCollins Publishers Inc.

In a Creepy, Creepy Place *and Other Scary Stories*
Text copyright © 1996 by Judith Gorog
Illustrations copyright © 1996 by Kimberly Bulcken Root
Library of Congress Cataloging-in-Publication Data
Gorog, Judith.
   In a creepy, creepy place and other scary stories / by Judith Gorog ;
illustrations by Kimberly Bulcken Root.
   p.   cm.
   Contents: Take out the trash — Frankenflopper — The scary place
— Gar —My good angel.
   Summary: A collection of scary stories with unpredictable events
and bizarre characters.
   ISBN 0-06-025131-X. — ISBN 0-06-025132-8 (lib. bdg.)
   ISBN 0-06-442057-4 (pbk.)
   1. Horror tales, American.   2. Children's stories, American.
[1. Horror stories.   2. Short stories.]   I. Root, Kimberly Bulcken, ill.
II. Title.
PZ7.G673In   1996   96-21713
[Fic]—dc20   CIP
                                                                    AC
Typography by Nancy Sabato
❖
First Harper Trophy edition, 1997

For Nikki—
her own book

Contents

In a Creepy, Creepy Place and Other Scary Stories

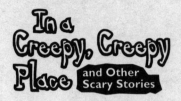

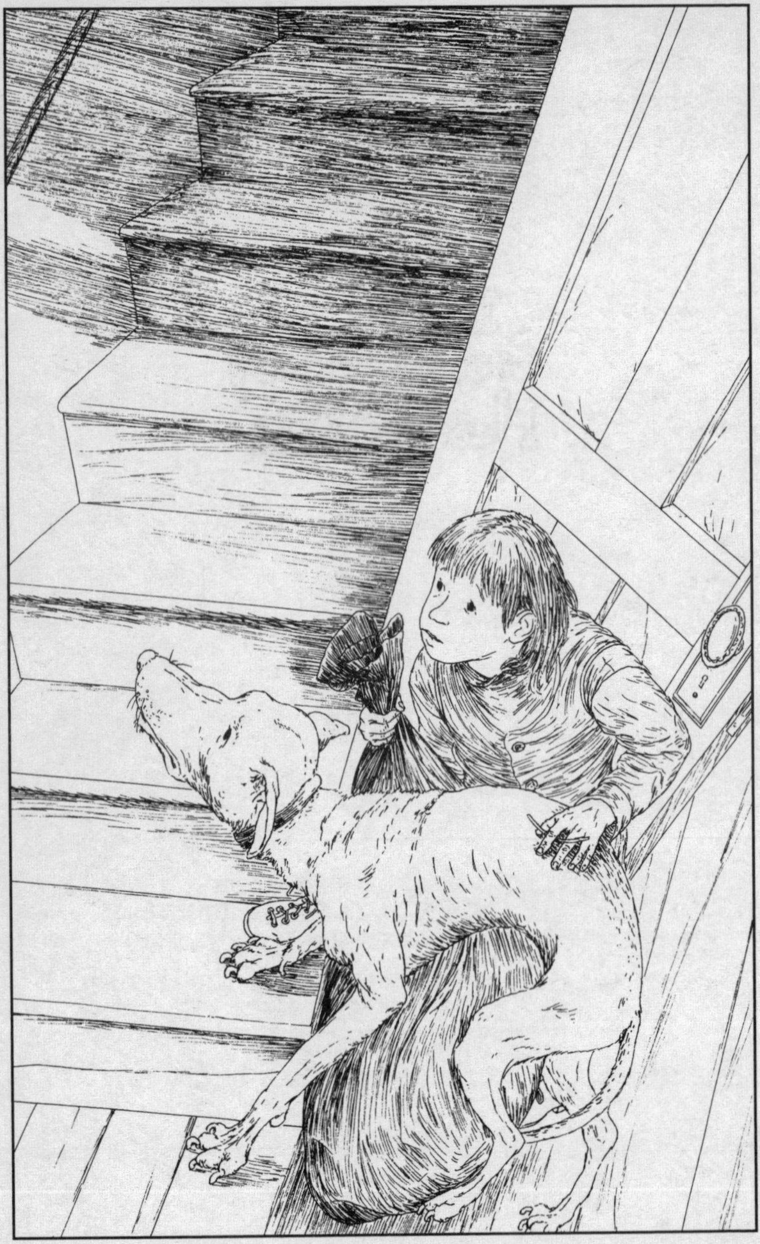

Take Out the Trash

Sophia had a problem, a new and very big problem. Thinking about it was keeping her awake, even though she was supposed to be having fun sleeping over at her best friend's house.

But, as luck had it, that very same night, while her friend Devon was asleep in the next bed, a nightmare gave Sophia the answer.

Suddenly, in the deep darkness, Devon's little brother shouted and cried. Sophia sat up. Devon woke up. They could hear the little brother sobbing, a door opening, footsteps in the hall. Sophia followed Devon, who followed her parents into her little brother's bedroom.

"When you have a bad dream," Devon's mom said, with the little brother in her lap, "and you are feeling afraid . . ."

"You get a friend," said Devon's dad.

"A friend?" The little brother's face right away looked more interested than scared.

"Yup. You dream yourself a friend to help you."

Sophia listened, thinking about her problem. A friend would be good help, and best of all, she knew just which friend to get. Not a dream friend, but a real one.

Sophia's problem was the trash. Just like that, out of the blue, Sophia's mom had said that she, Sophia, was now old enough to do a big, important job for the family.

"You can collect all the wastepaper baskets and empty them into the trash."

Sophia, who was a quick thinker, had asked, *"All?"*

"Of course," her mother had replied.

Sophia had nearly choked.

You see, taking out the trash in Sophia's house was a problem for Sophia because the staircase to the second floor creaked no matter how carefully she stepped on it. The stair creaked, "Gonna getcha, eek!"

Also, even with the lights on in the staircase and in the second-floor hall, shadows lurked in the doorways. The shadows jumped back when Sophia turned on a light, but she could hear them whisper, "Don't come here."

Collecting the wastepaper baskets on the second floor was a job that made your heart beat so you could hear it along with the sounds of the old house. Sophia's own bedroom was on the second floor. Sometimes she had to go up alone to brush her teeth before her mom or dad came to say good night. Those times she stomped hard on every step so she could not hear the "Gonna getcha, eek!" from the stair. She stomped hard along the hallway to her room, so she could not hear the shadows whisper, "Don't come here."

"What *is* that up there, elephants?" Sophia's dad would call.

Sophia always laughed. She knew that making noise covered up the monster voices and made her feel brave. She knew that even in her room there could be things waiting under the bed to grab her ankles. She made noise and she turned on lights, and she was brave on the second floor after dark.

At the bottom of the third-floor staircase was a wooden door that stayed shut. Even with the door closed, Sophia could picture what was behind it. The third-floor staircase was narrow. The steps were taller than the steps to the second floor.

The plaster on the walls of the steep, narrow third-floor staircase was full of mean eyes. Those eyes stared at you when you weren't watching, and blinked shut as soon as you turned to look.

Down on the second floor, Sophia could hear the music her parents played in the living room. She could even hear the dishwasher if the kitchen door was open. Up on the third floor, it was as if the rest of the house were gone.

On the third-floor staircase Sophia heard only the creak of the steps, felt the watching of the mean eyes. And, up on the third floor, there was laughter and rattling you only heard on the third floor. The third-floor steps creaked, "You'll never get back down." The windows tapped out, "Too late. Too late." Inside the three rooms the air was cold on your neck, and in your ears were many laughing voices, taunting, "Nyeh-nyeh-nyeh-nyeh-nyeh."

How could Sophia go up there to collect the trash? It was not a place to be even in the daytime, so far from the rest of the house, so far from anybody except the monsters that lived there.

All the trash.

Get a friend.

Sophia's best friend in all the world lived right in the kitchen. Sophia's best friend in all the world would do whatever Sophia asked. Sophia's best friend was big enough to go up to the third floor, up the steep, terrifying third floor staircase. She was big enough to face monsters.

Yes. That was definitely a good idea, to get a friend to help when you were scared.

When trash collecting night came,

Sophia went into the kitchen and called her best friend.

"Come, Posy! Come! Good dog."

Posy, tail wagging, pink tongue showing in her doggie grin, got up and followed Sophia.

"Come, girl! Come." Up the staircase they went, to the second floor. Posy's doggie nails sounded *click-click* on the staircase. It was great to have a good friend along. With Posy panting and Posy clicking, Sophia could barely hear the staircase say "Gonna getcha, eek!"

At the top of the stairs, Posy waited for Sophia to turn on the lights. Posy waited for Sophia to go into the rooms to collect the wastebaskets. Sophia noticed Posy hanging back. Sophia put the baskets in a row in the hall.

"Come! Posy! Good girl!" Sophia called. She waited. Sophia wanted to go faster, but Posy walked very slowly toward the door to the third floor.

At the first screeching twist of the doorknob, Posy turned and *click-click*ed her doggie claws down the second-floor hall, without a backward glance. "Posy! Come!" ordered Sophia, but Posy started down the stairs. Sophia grabbed the second-floor baskets and followed Posy. She emptied the baskets into the trash cans, called Posy, and started back up the stairs. Posy was not exactly close behind her.

"Don't forget the third floor," called Sophia's mother.

Sophia made Posy come into every room while she put away the second-floor baskets. She made Posy heel as they approached the third-floor door, which Sophia had left open.

"You'll never get back down," groaned the staircase. Right and left, the eyes on the walls blinked. "Nyeh-nyeh-nyeh-nyeh-nyeh," laughed the voices from upstairs. "Too late. Too late," rapped out the windows.

Well, Sophia does have a friend with her when she goes up that groaning staircase to the third floor. She has Posy in her arms while the eyes stare and blink. She has Posy between her feet while the shadows reach out from the chilly rooms. With Sophia dragging a trash bag *and* pushing and pulling and coaxing and calling, Posy helps get the trash every week. It is not easy, this having a real friend help you. It only works because Sophia has said it out loud, and she means it: Sophia will leave Posy *alone* on the third floor if she does not come along to get the job done.

Worst of all, the monsters on the third floor laugh and laugh.

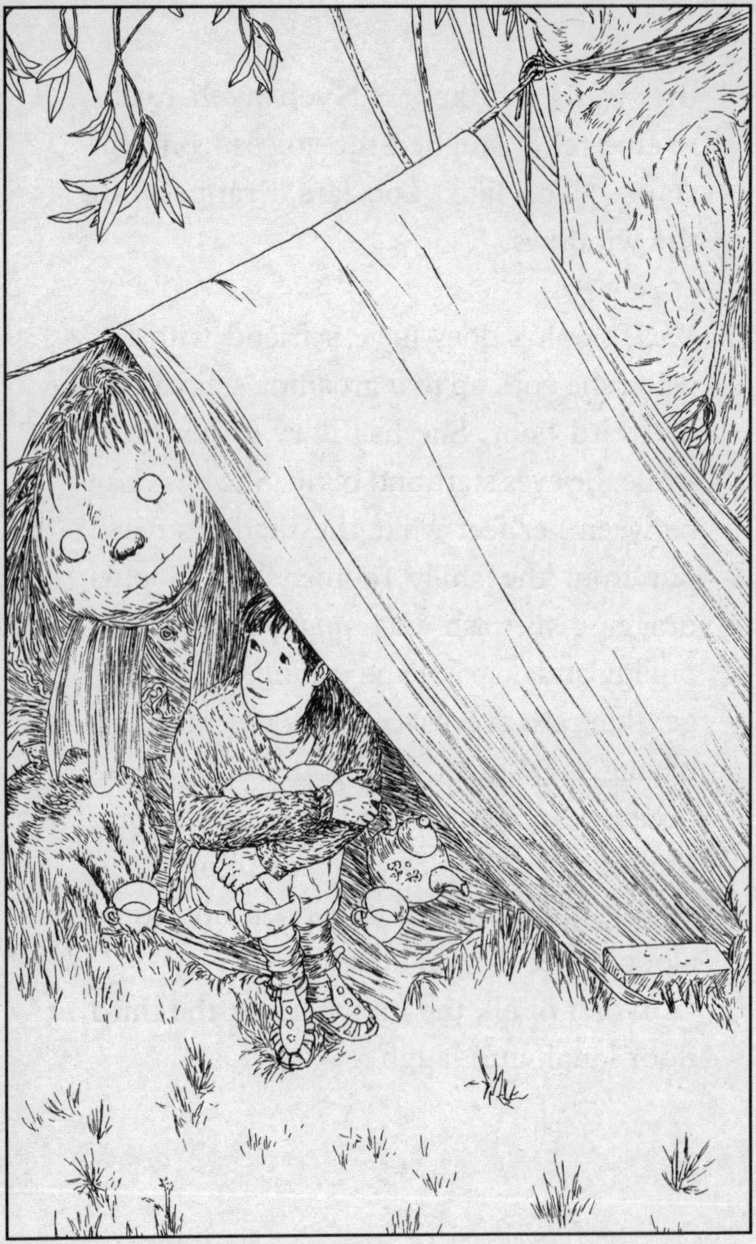

Frankenflopper

"Please, please!" Jessie must have said the word fifteen times, but the big kids did not answer. They did not open the door of the TV room, but they did turn up the volume on the set. Jessie sank to the hall floor. They had told her she was too little to watch the movie. They had pushed her out of the room, and they had shut the door. They yelled that she had to go to bed, and they did not open the door even when she said please. But they had turned up the volume to drown out the sound of her. That, at least, was good news because she could hear the movie quite clearly.

Jessie put her eye to the keyhole. What

was this movie that she was too little to watch?

Jessie could hear, and through the keyhole she could see the TV screen. For a long time she listened and watched, and for the life of her she could not imagine why the big kids said the movie was scary.

The movie was pretty simple. A man who wanted a friend built himself a huge dolly. He did some stuff, and the dolly came to life.

Jessie yawned. The big kids made no sense at all.

Jessie awoke early the next morning, in her bed. She stretched and yawned. She did not remember crawling into bed, and she did not remember the end of the movie the big kids had been watching.

Nobody else was awake. Jessie climbed quietly out of bed. One thing about the movie had been good. Making a friend was not a bad idea at all. Rummaging through the toy box, she found old dress-up clothes, more than one broken dolly, parts of trucks, and four animals with stuffing leaking or an eye, an ear, or a foot missing.

From the basement Jessie brought up a big roll of duct tape. She got out her scissors and set to work.

By the time the rest of the family was awake, Jessie had made herself a wonderful, and truly enormous, friend.

At breakfast Mom asked, "Who's that?"

"What was the name in that movie?" Jessie said. "I want to name her something like that. Franken . . . Frank N.? Frannie N.? No. I remember. My friend is called Frankenflopper."

"Great," said Daddy. "Have some fruit."

One by one the other kids came to breakfast.

"Euhhh, gross! Jessie, get that out of here!"

"Oh no. Those eyes. I'm not eating with that in here."

"Eeeeeek!! What *is* that thing?"

"Mommmm! Make Jessie take *that* outta here!"

Jessie was overjoyed. Old Frankenflopper made the big kids freak out.

The rest of the day went pretty well. The big kids and their friends all came to the doorway of Jessie's room, where she and Frankenflopper were telling stories in a tent. The big kids were too scared to come into the room.

The next day some of Jessie's friends came over. That was not so great.

"Jessie, put it in the closet, please."

"Jessie, those eyes stare at me."

"Jessie, let's go to my house. Uh, and can you leave that monster at home?"

Jessie did not care. She could play with her friends, or she could play with Frankenflopper, who had more and better ideas than most of the kids anyway.

Life might have gone on that way forever, except for what happened one summer afternoon. Jessie and Frankenflopper were in a tent they'd made under the clothesline. Mom and Dad walked past, on their way to the hammock and chairs under the big oak tree at the back of the garden.

Mom shuddered. "Have you noticed the eyes on that thing?"

Dad agreed. "Mmmm. Creepy."

The two friends pretended not to hear. Jessie made herself be extra cheerful and gave Frankenflopper all the best parts of the game. But that night Frankenflopper ran away.

Jessie was really worried. What if Frankenflopper toppled into a storm drain? What if she got chased by wild dogs? What if the weather turned violent and she got struck by lightning? What if on a foggy road a big truck ran over her?

Nobody else cared. Nobody helped Jessie look.

Jessie walked over the whole neighborhood, faster and faster, until her side hurt. Along the way she asked everyone about Frankenflopper.

No luck.

She walked, looking behind bushes, up in trees, under cars.

It was getting dark. Jessie knew she had to go back home.

The huge door of old Granny Grinder's garage was closed, but the rusty padlock hung open. Pulling the door ajar, Jessie peered into the darkness. She had to wait a minute before she could see. Inside were the lumpy, black shadows of old cars and twisted snow blowers. The window, thick with spiderwebs, was crowded with buckets and tools on the sill. On the walls hung ropes and forks, shovels and rakes. Baskets unraveled in one corner. A broken ladder leaned against the fourth wall. Jessie looked up at the rafters above the ladder.

Two yellow eyes glowed down at her. Two huge tears plopped into the dust on the floor. Someone snuffled. Jessie heard the sound of a nose being wiped on a sleeve.

"Flop. I know your yellow eyes. Come down and come home, or we are going to get into big trouble."

Frankenflopper tumbled down the ladder, stumbled across the floor.

Jessie only had time to give her a fast

hug, because it was deeply dark by then, and they had to run home. It was not easy, with Frankenflopper blubbering the whole way.

After supper Jessie closed her bedroom door and sat down on the floor with Frankenflopper.

"Look. You're my friend. I like being with you. I don't even care if the others are afraid of you. But if you want to be less scary, should I cut you down? Should I make you smaller?" Jessie didn't like that idea herself.

But Frankenflopper absolutely wailed at the question. It took her forever to be reassured. She kept looking around to see if Jessie had scissors hidden somewhere.

"Okay, okay. What about how they say you stare?"

"Sunglasses?" sniffled Frankenflopper.

They tried the sunglasses. They tried

a lot of things. Nothing worked, until the big kids and Jessie and her friends all got taller and taller. When they were the same size as Frankenflopper, they weren't afraid any longer.

But Jessie's parents stayed scared of those yellow eyes.

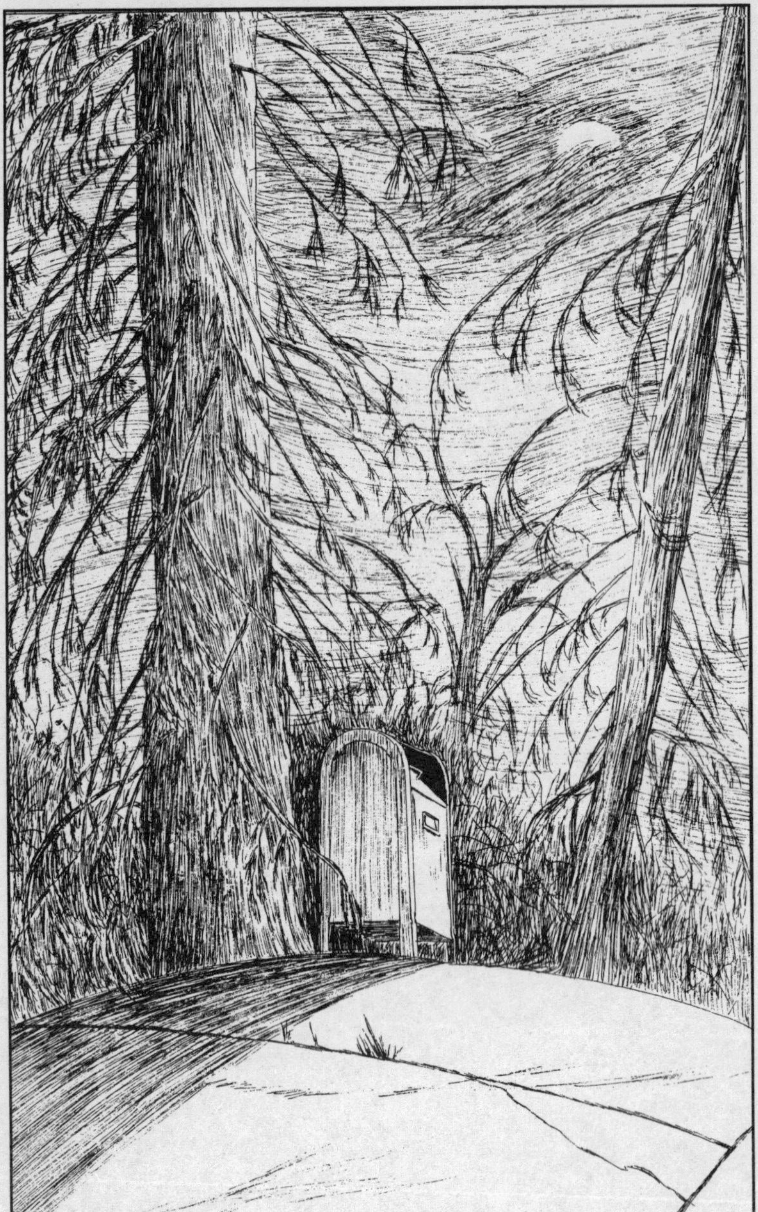

The Scary Place

Not everybody knew about the scary place. Casey, Jay, and Briggs did; they passed it every day. For those three friends, the scary place was not the moldy, peeling house with the shutter that banged in the wind. It was not the yard where a huge dog ran along the fence, its hair standing on end, flecks of froth flying from its fangs as it snarled and lunged at them. No, and it was not the house where the angry man yelled that he would telephone their parents or bellowed that he'd have them arrested.

The angry man stood on his porch, the veins of his face and neck throbbing as he shouted the whole time they passed, when they had not done anything, not even dragged sticks along his black iron fence.

Those places could be scary sometimes, but nothing matched the real, true scary place.

It was a corner, with a mailbox that made a huge shadow, even on dark days. The branches of a towering evergreen tree scraped the sidewalk. The air smelled of dead things, and the wind whispered secrets, even on the stillest, hottest day of June.

Casey, Jay, and Briggs passed the scary place twice a day, the whole year of third grade. They could have gone another way to school and home, but never did.

They passed the scary place in silence, each one holding his breath, eyes straight ahead, looking at the sidewalk. They were sure that if they did not breathe in the air under the tree, if they did not hear the rustling from inside the mailbox, and if they did not see the things that surely lurked around that corner, they would be safe. At least that time.

Sometimes one of them even got sent to the scary place by a mom or dad or grandmother to mail a letter in the dark. That was bad. That was when you tried to get your sister or brother or a friend to go with you. Better still, you tried to get someone to go instead of you.

At night, the mailbox loomed tall, its shadow twisting along the ground. The dark branches of the tree scraped and scratched the earth; they sawed the sky.

On the ground, up the trunk, and out on the twigs, invisible beasts scrabbled and crunched. You told yourself that it had to be the wind that made the mailbox howl and moan. Still, the sounds made your skin move in a most uncomfortable way.

Not everybody knew about the scary place; but Casey, Jay, and Briggs did. They knew the shapes and shadows and sounds of that old mailbox. They knew the smell of dead things. They feared the moisture dripping from the tree and shivered at the secret whispering in the branches. Worst of all, night or day, rain or shine, when you approached that corner, the tree blocked your view,
    so you were never quite prepared
    when some big kid hiding there

jumped
     out,
         shrieking
             BOO!

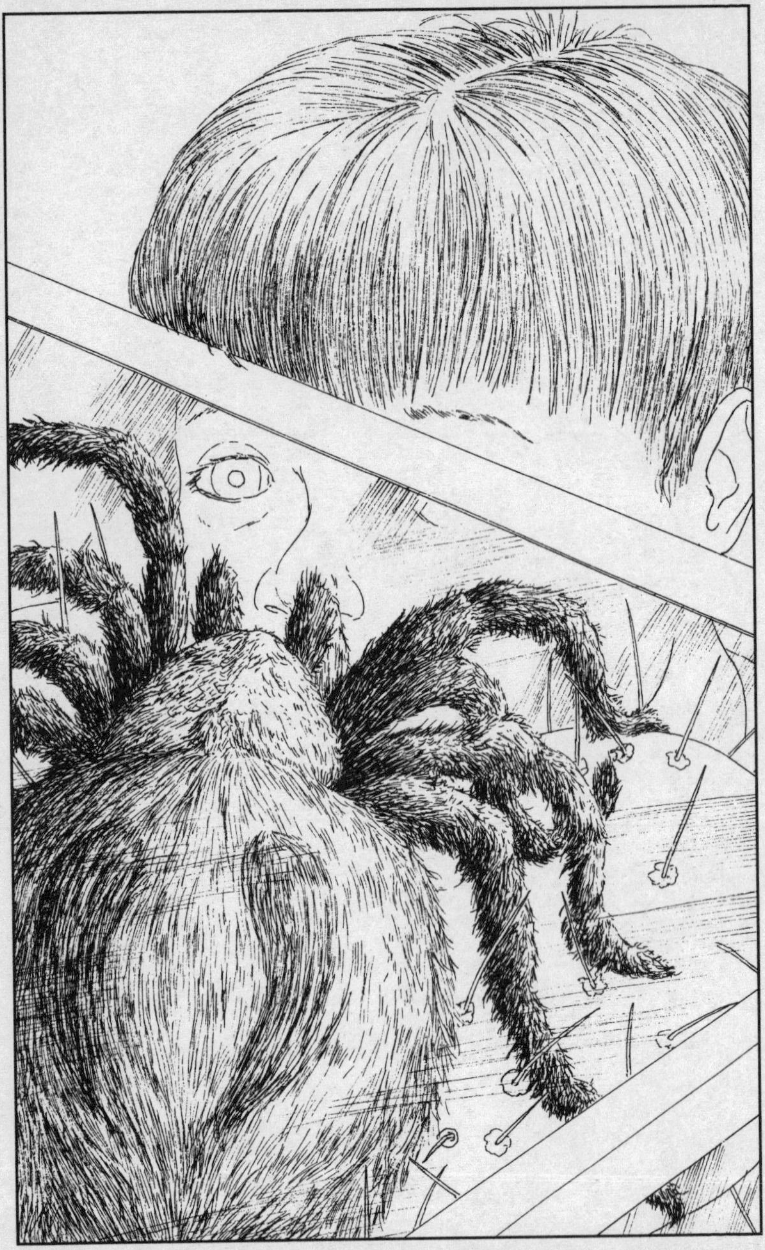

Gar

By the time he was ten years old, Gar had loved, and occasionally lost, most of the usual pets. Gar liked all animals, but he liked the usual pets best when something exciting happened. Gar loved it when somehow his two gerbils multiplied until there were thirty-five. And it was great when sixteen of them chewed their way out of the cardboard box Gar had put them in, and got between the walls of the house. Gar and his mom could hear the gerbils running, up and down and all around inside the walls.

Gar's mom was thinking how to get the sixteen gerbils back, when they heard another sound. The neighbor's cat was in there, chasing them.

Sometimes sad things happened, like the time Gar had a brand-new white mouse. He had barely named it when it somehow got out of its cage and ran downstairs. As it streaked across the hall floor, Gar's dog sauntered over, snapped up the mouse in one gulp, and swallowed it before Gar could say a word.

But good things happened, too, with the usual pets. Gar's fat old hamster, Spike, escaped once for six days. By the time Gar's mom found him, Spike had made two different nests. Gar thought the nests were amazingly complete. There was bedding shredded fine, and food Spike must have foraged from the supply in Gar's bedroom.

But Gar's mom was mad that the nests were in handmade decorator pillows. Gar's mom started insisting that Gar do a better job of keeping his pets in their cages. She said if Gar wanted to live with animals loose, he should go, as soon as he was grown up, to a place where he could join the animals in their freedom.

Gar looked around his house. What was life with an old cat, an old dog, an old parakeet, and an old hamster? What Gar needed was a real pet: a young python, rattlesnake, or tarantula. But when he casually mentioned getting a python, a rattlesnake, or a tarantula, Gar's mother replied, "No. No. Period. You already lead a life that is too dangerous for my taste. I'd like to see you live long enough to become an adult. Then get whatever pet you want!"

Gar was certain his mother had an obsession with his growing up.

Gar did not want to wait to be a grown-up. He wanted a new pet, something exciting, and right away. Why did his mother think anything he did was dangerous? Mostly it was barely fun.

That was it. Gar decided he wanted a really huge and very hairy spider. He scorned the smaller wolf spiders. No way. Gar was determined to own only one sort, the largest of the South American tarantulas, a ten-inch spider with meaningful venom. Gar chose that one after hearing his friend K.C. describe in detail the agonies of a guy who thrust his hand into a bunch of bananas. A tarantula in the middle of the bunch bit the guy. It was a ghastly death.

Gar, who never gave up easily, did not tell his mother a single scary tarantula story. Instead, he started reading up on the care and feeding of tarantulas. As he read, Gar planned the convincing of his mother. First, he needed a young pet. Second, he needed a ten-inch South American tarantula.

Gar had not begun when his mother surprised him right out of a good mood.

Gar's mother asked did Gar know that Mr. Fredericks at Exotic Pets had a tarantula?

Now, Gar had reason to be suspicious of his mom because she earned her living through illusion. She made stage props: scepters, swords and shields, goblets that appeared to be encrusted with jewels. She made corpses when necessary. Everything she made had to look real and cost next to nothing. Consequently, Gar's mother was a great shopper, a great scrounger, and most of all, a great faker.

Yes, indeed. Gar was suspicious. Why did she mention tarantulas *before* he had begun to convince her? Why? Had his mother made some tarantula robot and put it in the shop to fool him?

Caught off balance, unable to decide how to respond, Gar did the best he could. He picked a fight with his mother.

"Tarantula?" he sputtered. "It's probably some wimpy wolf spider! Tarantulas can live for twenty years! You're just telling me it's there to make me feel bad!"

Gar's mother did not point out that his statements made no sense. She took the dog's leash from the peg near the back door, then waved good-bye as she closed the screen. "I'm off for a walk with the dog. See you in an hour or so."

Gar's mother had refused to quarrel.

Muttering, Gar set off. He went through the yards of the most vicious dogs in town. He walked on the fences or cut across the lawns of every mean person he'd ever heard of. You could follow his route by the sounds of angry dogs and threatening humans.

The journey, which was not the shortest way to the pet store, calmed him. He arrived smiling. The tarantula, alone in a glass terrarium with a heavy mesh cover on top, returned Gar's stare with tranquility.

He was big.

"Yup. South American. A bird-eating spider. Fella breeds 'em for zoos. *Avicularia*. Technically not a tarantula. Handsome, ain't he?" Mr. Fredericks ambled back to the cash register to ring up some lizards.

For hours Gar sat staring at the spider. He was amazing, the best. Man, look at those legs. Look at that body! He was no robot Gar's mom had constructed to fool Gar. This spider was real.

After a while, Gar felt they were brothers. It was as if he could see into the spider's mind. Yeah.

The tarantula was thinking, Now is this the one? Will I be living with this guy, in his room? And Gar was thinking, Would you like that? If you would, how can I convince my mom? And the spider was thinking, Your mom? Is she the one who was here looking at the colors of flamingo feathers? And Gar was thinking, Yeah, that's my mom. And the two of them were thinking, How can we convince her?

The spider was thinking Gar's mom could be convinced. The spider was thinking that he had already put it into Gar's mom's mind to tell. She should tell she'd seen him, *if* she had the right sort of kid at home, a kid that might be in tune with a tarantula. And Gar thought, Yeah, good suggestion, because she did mention you.

The spider was thinking that Gar's mom could be convinced if maybe she came back to the Exotic Pets store. Gar thought he could get her back into the store to see exotic birds, something too expensive to buy but interesting to her. Gar would not talk about tarantulas to get his mother to return.

Reluctantly, Gar went home. He went

the short way, which was not so interesting but dirty because he had to crawl
through a tunnel. The next day he did
not say that he had been to the pet shop.
Instead, he said that his friend K.C. had
told him there were some cool new exotic
birds in Mr. Fredericks' shop.

Gar did not say a word about the
tarantula, but he did count his money
and clean under the couch cushions to
see what he could add to it.

One day later, Gar went back to the
shop. The spider was there, pacing in a
terrarium Gar thought was too small.
After they greeted each other, the spider
stopped his walking. Gar thought again
how awesome he was. Huge.

The spider addressed Gar. "Your
mom thinks you need a guardian angel."

"Me?" Gar snorted.

"If it works, why knock it?" The tarantula chuckled.

"Whaddya mean?"

"Looking at me, your mother was thinking how she keeps praying for a guardian angel for you. She worries that you like danger too much. She was thinking that if you had a spider with venom, she would never sleep. Then she was wishing I were a guardian angel in the shape of a spider, just the sort of angel you'd need to keep you safe. It seemed a good idea. So I hinted to her that she had guessed correctly."

"She believed you?"

"Maybe. If nobody else buys me, she might do it."

"You," suggested Gar, "should make everyone who comes in here feel really scared of you, until I help convince her."

The tarantula agreed it was a good idea.

Gar went home, taking a shortcut over the roofs of the neighbors' garages. To convince his mom he deserved the spider, he emptied the trash, including the kitchen garbage, without being asked. He then went to his room, where he read some more about the care, feeding, and breeding of *Avicularia*.

For two long, agonizing days, Gar was cheerful and helpful. He tried to think of ways he could use the words "safe" and "tarantula" in the same sentence.

Finally, at supper, his mom asked, "Did you ever go see that tarantula?"

"He's cool." Gar grinned.

"I've been back to the shop three times since I first saw it," Gar's mom said. "Mr. Fredericks has been saving me some amazing feathers. Anyway, the spider seems calm. Are you sure you won't be bored? A spider doesn't do much as long as it stays in its terrarium. Agreed?"

"You mean you'll let me get him?"

"Mr. Fredericks likes you. He'll sell him to you for cost."

Gar sat in amazement. It worked! The

plan worked, like the answer to a prayer.

"You know, Mom, they aren't vicious. They only bite if they are scared."

"Please. Even so. Don't let him loose. Promise?"

"Sure, Mom."

Gar called him Killer.

Every morning Gar opened his eyes with joy. There was Killer, just a pane of glass away. There, living in a terrarium next to Gar's bed, was the most terrifying spider any of his friends, any of the kids in town, had ever seen.

It was great.

Great until the night Gar awoke and walked barefoot to the kitchen.

His mom was drinking coffee at the kitchen table, drinking coffee and talking to someone standing there. That someone stood nine feet tall, with wings that touched the ceiling. When Gar said, "What?" the someone vanished. Gar's mom was in the kitchen alone. She looked at Gar and smiled at him, as if she had been alone the whole time.

Gar ran back to check his room. Killer was in the terrarium. But. But. But. Had Gar dreamed a nine-foot-tall angel in the kitchen?

Killer was silent, as if asleep.

Gar sat thinking hard. Well, then. If Killer really was a guardian angel in disguise, if that angel made his mom think Gar was always safe, always protected— well, then.

Gar sat thinking and smiling. Did this mean his mom would let him get a room full of pit vipers? And if she did, would it be any fun?

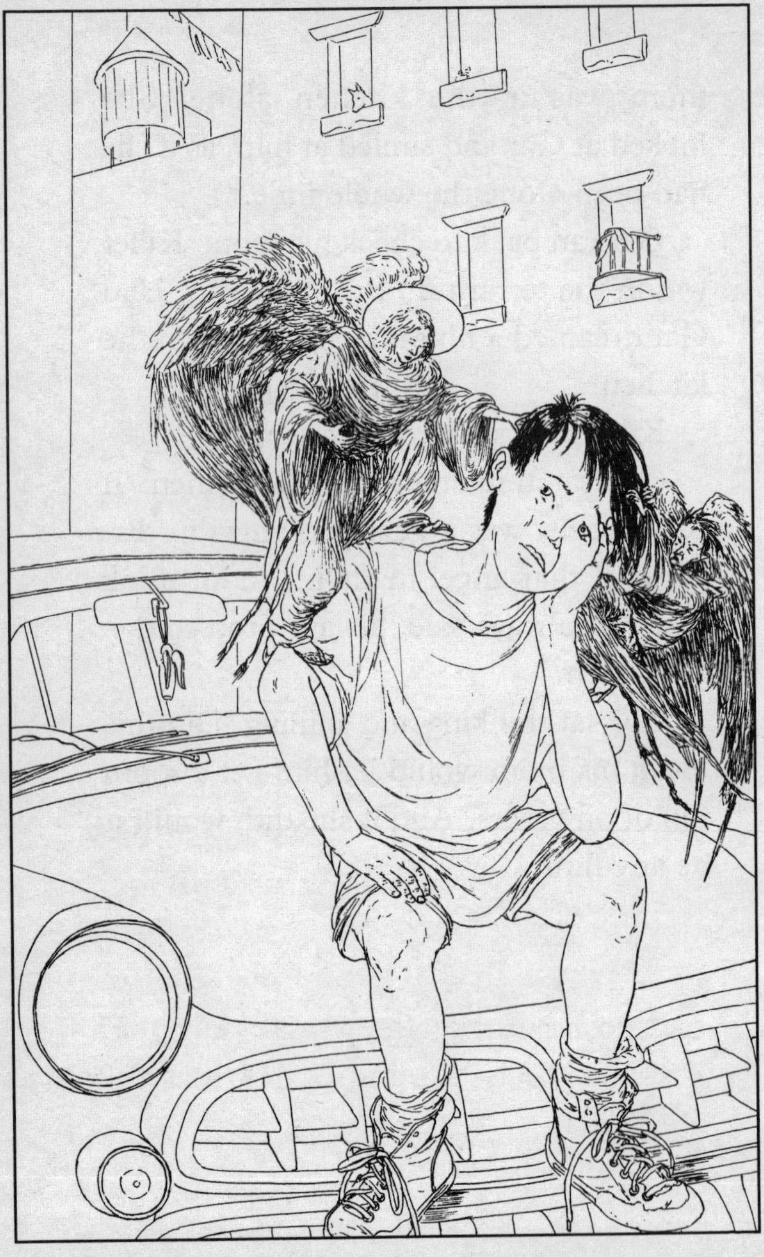

My Good Angel

"You are a good boy, Hector," my grand-mother always says to me, giving my right shoulder a little squeeze. "You listen to that good angel on your shoulder, when he whispers into your ear to help you with difficult decisions. Good boy," she whispers, and smiles at me.

My grandmother knows it is not easy, not easy at all. You see, I don't only have to resist the voice of the wicked angel on my other shoulder, when he suggests bad things I could do and what fun they would be. My biggest problem, and getting bigger, is taking care of my little sister, Rosita Angelique. She is only four years old, but big and strong like you never saw. People think she is eight and me the little kid. My job is to keep that kid out of trouble.

In the morning, I walk her to nursery school, on the way to my school. Last Monday we set out. She was tugging at my hand. We walked. I had to keep her from running into the street, which was a struggle all the way. Then, with the whole city dry and not a cloud in the sky, how could there be, on our way to school, a puddle that gigantic? I saw it, but too late to change the way we went. Besides, I'd be late for school. I started talking to her.

"Listen, Rosita, you can't go in that dirty, greasy puddle. Not on the way to school."

I was trying to be calm, but my little sister was pulling on me. She was heading, fast as anything, straight for that puddle. In my left ear, my wicked angel was flapping his wings, hollering at me, "Just leave her right here. You are going to be late for school. Just leave her here, right in the water. Leave!"

And in my right ear, my good angel said, "Use your head, Hector."

I did. My little sister cannot arrive at school with wet shoes and socks, I thought, but she can walk in the puddle with bare feet. Because she is so horse-and-pony strong, I had to talk fast, telling her what we would do and how she could walk the whole length of the puddle, the whole way.

Now, I never know with my little sister just what her angels are telling her, because she is a pistol; I'll tell you that. But this time she listened to me. I got her shoes and socks off, and she walked the length of the puddle, getting only a little mud and greasy water on her rolled-up pants. Whew. I even got to school on time. But I wonder if her shoes were on the wrong feet. I say that because my bad angel was laughing something awful in my left ear when I let go of Rosita's sweaty hand at the door of her school.

On Wednesday, my grandmother made a cake from a recipe in a magazine. That cake was three layers high, with jam in between the layers, and it had some frosting, and it was, I tell you honestly, a beautiful sight. My grandmother went to get the laundry from the lines on the roof, and my little sister, who is only four years old, took the middle layer from that cake, without making even much mess, and started eating it. I came into the kitchen too late to stop her.

My bad angel told me to grab some and eat it. My good angel said, "Hector, that is a bad idea." I turned my back on my little sister and the cake she was eating while I was trying to make up my mind. Good thing, too, because my grandmother came back into the kitchen and caught her, and I got a double helping of cake after dinner and Rosita for once got nothing. Only trouble was, I did not like that magazine cake.

That is how the days and nights pass. I baby-sit my little sister.

Today I am so sleepy. Last night I had to put Rosita Angelique to bed, and I wanted more than anything to watch the television. Everyone was at work, and it was my job, and so I started putting her to bed. But she was not in the mood.

My bad angel told me flat out to slug her a few times and then she would cry. "Hector," said the bad angel. "It only takes minutes for her to cry herself to sleep." He said it over and over again.

But my good angel was telling me in a quiet voice, "Hector, if you hit her, then you hurt her, and that is wrong, and what is more, my friend Hector, if you teach her to hit, well, then, just think about it. Right now your little sister is nearly taller than you and nearly heavier than you and she is growing like mad and you are not growing at all, my man, so think about what could happen if you teach her to hit all the time."

I did not hit her, and I was patient, but it took a long time to get her to sleep. Then, to give myself a reward, I watched the television. Yeah, I admit it; I watched too late. This afternoon I must baby-sit my little sister, and I am so sleepy.

Rosita wants to pretend to drive Papi's car. It is parked on the street in front of our building. It would be better to be out on the sidewalk playing, or in the building. It would be better to be almost anywhere except sitting in the sun in the hotter-than-an-oven car, but Rosita will not listen to me. She is pretending to drive, and I am trying to stay awake.

My bad angel tells me to go inside, where it is cool. He says I should take a nap and leave the brat here.

My good angel tells me I have to stay on the job.

I am staying. That's why my grandmother smiles at me. That's why she gives me special treats and tells me what a good man I am.

But, ahh, I am so sleepy.

I admit it. I fell asleep in that hot car. I dreamed we were bumping along, bumping along, going somewhere. I dreamed I was on a trip, just bumping along, not so smooth but a little jerky, and then pretty smooth, and then a jolt. My dream got quiet then. I dreamed of picnicking under trees of green leaves. All of a sudden my little sister started poking me in the arm, hard.

"What is it?" I looked out the car window. We were stopped on a street of big trees. We were on a street of big trees, in the car, with my little sister in the driver's seat.

"Hector. The car stopped. Make it go, Hector. Make it go."

I looked around. I got out of the car. I could see the street signs. I could see the car jammed up against the curb.

My little sister had driven the car ten whole city blocks! A four-year-old kid!

I looked around. Whew. No damage. I got back into the car.

In my left ear, I could hear the voice of my bad angel insisting, "Hector. Drive that car!"

And in my right ear? For once my two angels agreed. Because in my right ear, my good angel said, "Hector. You cannot permit a four-year-old child to drive that car home."